One brave little angel

The Archangel of Courage touched the Little Angel of Courage on the cheek. "Do you think you can help Paul?"

The Little Angel of Courage looked at Paul. Earning her wings, one feather at a time, was hard—but that was the pace she liked. After all, there was something about the whole idea of flying around as an archangel that made her stomach flutter.

But she was sure she could help this boy, and if she could help him, well, then, she should.

Aladdin
Angelwings
No. 4

One Leap
Forward

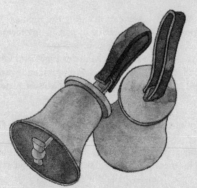

Donna Jo Napoli
illustrations by Lauren Klementz-Harte

Aladdin Paperbacks

Thank you to all my family,
Brenda Bowen, Nöelle Paffett-Lugassy, and Richard Tchen

First Aladdin Paperbacks edition December 1999

Aladdin Paperbacks
An imprint of Simon & Schuster
Children's Publishing Division
1230 Avenue of the Americas
New York, NY 10020

Library of Congress Cataloging-in-Publication Data
Napoli, Donna Jo, 1948–
One leap forward / Donna Jo Napoli ; illustrations by
Lauren Klementz-Harte. — 1st Aladdin Paperbacks ed.
p.   cm. — (Aladdin angelwings ; 4)
Summary: The Little Angel of Courage helps a young boy gain
enough confidence in himself to take ballet lessons, even though his
best friend makes fun of him.
ISBN 0-689-82986-8 (pbk.)
[1. Angels—Fiction. 2. Courage—Fiction. 3. Self-confidence—Fiction.
4. Ballet dancing—Fiction.]
I. Klementz-Harte, Lauren, 1961– ill. II. Title. III. Series: Napoli,
Donna Jo, 1948–
Aladdin angelwings ; 4.
PZ7.N150t   1999
[Fic]—dc21   99-23980
CIP

For my boys,
who know how to dance

Aladdin

Angelwings

№ 4

One Leap Forward

Angel Talk

W atch closely now," said the Archangel of Courage.

The Little Angel of Courage watched the girls in their tutus. She looked for anyone who was hesitating or hanging back. But all of them were paying attention to the ballet teacher and all of them tried every move the teacher demonstrated. "I don't see anyone who needs courage," said the little angel.

The Archangel of Courage smiled knowingly. "Look harder."

A tall girl held her chin high. A short girl held her back straight. A blond girl was sweating, but smiling, too. A redhead had determination written all over her face. The Little Angel of Courage looked hard at each girl. No one looked timid. Instead, they looked cheerful

in their blue leotards, like a row of cornflowers on a spring morning.

The girls turned to the barre. They hurried in crisscrossing paths to their spots. The little angel could see that they had fixed spots at the barre: They were arranged according to height. As the third little girl in the line turned, she gave a quick wave.

A boy on the other side of the room jumped to his feet and waved back wildly. Then he sat down on the observation bench and stared, both legs swinging under him, his lips slightly parted.

The girls put one leg on the barre and both arms above their head in an arc.

The boy on the bench reached his arms above his head in an arc, too.

The girls stood with one hand on the barre now and kicked one leg, toe pointed to the side.

The boy stretched his legs out in front of him on the bench and pointed his toes.

3

The girls put both hands on the barre and arched backward.

The boy arched backward. Farther and farther. So far, he fell off the bench with a crash.

The class looked at him.

The boy hopped back onto the bench and sat on his hands, not moving. He looked at his knees.

"I understand," said the Little Angel of Courage. "What's his name?"

"Paul. He comes to ballet class every Tuesday afternoon and watches his sister dance. He imitates all her moves." The Archangel of Courage touched the Little Angel of Courage on the cheek. "You need only five more feathers to fill out your wings and you'll be an archangel. I'm sure this job is worth a lot of feathers. Do you think you can help Paul?"

The Little Angel of Courage looked at Paul. Earning her wings, one feather at a time, was hard—but that was the pace she liked. After all, there was something about the whole idea of flying around as an archangel that made her stomach flutter in a sick way. Once she was an archangel, she'd have to guide little angels, and she wasn't sure at all that she knew how to do that yet.

But she was sure she could help this boy, and if she could help him, well, then, she should. Maybe she could do this job in only four feathers, so then she'd have a little more time before the bell rang announcing that she'd earned her wings—a little more time before she had to face becoming an archangel.

The Swan

Paul put his sneakers back on as he waited for his sister, Silvia, outside the dressing room. Older girls, in purple leotards, were already rushing out onto the wooden dance floor to warm up before the next lesson. Paul pressed against the wall to stay out of their way.

Silvia appeared beside him. "Let's go."

Paul followed her down the stairs of Camilla's School of Dance and out to the sidewalk.

"You fell off the bench today," said Silvia.

Paul already knew that. He walked a little faster.

"What were you doing?"

"Nothing."

Silvia hung her tote from her shoulder so

that her arms were free. She moved her arms in front of her as she walked.

"That's part of ballet, isn't it?" asked Paul. He swung his arms in a circle.

"Yup. These are called 'positions.'" Silvia glided along. Her arms streamed behind her now. Her head tilted forward gracefully.

Paul couldn't believe his eyes. "You're a swan."

"That's a nice thing to say. There's a famous ballet about a swan."

Paul remembered. He'd watched that ballet on TV. He had imagined he was the Prince.

"It's called *Swan Lake*. Someday I'm going to dance in that ballet." Silvia skipped ahead, and now she was his sister again, not a swan at all.

Paul swung his arms in a circle. "Am I the Prince?"

"Huh?" Silvia stopped and looked at Paul as though he were nuts. "What are you talking about?"

Paul felt stupid. Of course Silvia didn't think he was the Prince. Paul didn't know how to do ballet. He only knew how to do ordinary things, like run. He ran in a circle around Silvia, swinging his arms wildly. "These are my fastest sneakers."

"Who cares about speed? You don't have to be fast to do ballet." Silvia sniffed and did a little twirl. Her tote smacked against her knees.

Paul ran ahead of Silvia the rest of the way home.

Angel Talk

$\mathcal{S}$ ilvia isn't as graceful as she thinks," said the Little Angel of Courage. "In my opinion, Paul looked as much like a prince as she looked like a swan."

"Are you defending him?" The archangel smiled. "I'm glad you care so much about Paul already. But I don't think Silvia was trying to insult him. She doesn't know how he feels about ballet."

"She acts like she's the only one who knows anything about it, though."

"Well, she thinks she is." The Archangel of Courage moved her arms slowly in arcs, just like Silvia had.

"Paul knew about the Prince in *Swan Lake*."

"That's because he saw it on TV with his mother. It was that experience that made me notice him."

"He should have told Silvia," said the little angel. "And he should have explained what he meant when he asked her if he was the Prince."

"Well, little angel, it looks like you've found your first step in helping Paul to be courageous—getting him to speak up."

Pinch One

Paul turned off the TV and went to the kitchen table, where he'd left his notebook. He sat down.

"You can't sit here," said Silvia. "I'm doing my homework."

"I'm doing mine, too."

"No you're not. You were watching TV."

"TV's part of my homework. I had to watch the news for Current Events and find out one thing that happened in our country."

"That's dumb homework," said Silvia.

Paul agreed, but he decided not to tell Silvia. He wrote in his notebook.

"What did you write?" asked Silvia.

"The president visited China."

"That's not something that happened in our country. The president left the country to do it."

That was true. Paul tried to remember the rest of the news. He couldn't. He shut his notebook and watched Silvia.

"Don't watch me," said Silvia.

"Do you have a lot more to do?"

"Actually, I'm done." Silvia closed her notebook with a flourish. "Now I can practice ballet." She put her notebook in her backpack and put the backpack on the chair near the front door. Then she went into the living room and bent her knees outward.

Paul watched her from the hall.

Silvia glanced at him. "This is called a 'plié.'"

Paul moved into the part of the hall where Silvia couldn't see him. He did a plié. Then he went back to his first spot to watch again.

Silvia was on the floor with her back against the wall and her legs sticking straight out in front of her. She leaned forward till her chest rested on her legs.

"You never do that in class," said Paul.

Silvia looked at him. "This is home practice. The teacher told us to do it. It stretches
our hamstrings."

"Do I have hamstrings?"

"What? Everyone does. They're the mus-
cles down the backs of your thighs. Stop
bothering me. I have to concentrate."

Paul went back into his private area of the
hall and tried Silvia's hamstring stretch
against the wall. It was hard. He couldn't get
his head nearly as close to his knees as Silvia
could. Then he ran back to watch her again.

Silvia was on the floor on the other side of
the couch now. Paul couldn't see any of her
except her pointed toes.

Paul tiptoed halfway to the couch and
stopped. Maybe he should just go upstairs
and get ready for bed. He started to turn
around. "Ouch."

"What's the matter?" Silvia's head
popped up.

"Someone pinched me."

"Well, it wasn't me."

Paul grabbed his side where the pinch still stung. "Do you have to be in fifth grade to do ballet?"

"Of course not. I started only this year because I was too busy with swimming before. But Jennifer's little sister, Suzanne, takes ballet and she's in third grade, like you. And there are beginner classes for even smaller kids." Silvia stood up. "I'm done. And I get the shower first." She raced Paul up the stairs.

Angel Talk

"W̲ell, Paul asked the first important question," said the Archangel of Courage. "Were you part of that, or did he get up the gumption on his own?"

"Oh, I was definitely part of it," said the little angel. "Didn't you hear him say someone pinched him?"

"That was you?" The archangel smiled slowly. Then she burst out laughing. "A pinch of courage. I get it. What a funny little angel you are."

The little angel laughed, too. "It worked."

"It certainly did. And I think you deserve a feather for that."

A feather? The Little Angel of Courage sobered up fast. She hadn't thought that one little pinch would earn her a feather. Oh, dear.

Now she had only four feathers left to earn and she'd get her wings. She wasn't ready. She had better be a little more careful about giving out pinches.

Pinch Two

Paul added the numbers one more time. This was the second addition quiz of the year and it made him nervous. But the numbers kept adding up the same, so maybe he had the right answers. Finally, he stood up from his desk and walked to the front of the room. He handed his quiz sheet to Ms. Berkowitz.

"Thank you, Paul. You can go out to recess now."

Ms. Berkowitz was nice. She always gave them an extra recess on quiz days. As soon as you finished, you could go out onto the playground. But Ms. Berkowitz always allowed at least fifteen minutes outside after the very last person, so that everyone could have fun, even if they were slow at quizzes. She was fair that way.

Paul headed for the monkey bars. His best friend, Stephen, was already hanging upside down by his knees from the top. Stephen was a great climber. Paul laughed. "You look like a monster when you're upside down."

Stephen laughed back. "You always look like a monster. Come hang with me."

Paul reached for the bars. They were hot from the morning sun. He climbed up and hung beside Stephen. "We're like two bats."

"Vampire bats," said Stephen. "Whose blood should we suck?"

Paul surveyed the playground. There were lots of kids from another class in line for the swings. Even upside down, Paul could recognize Suzanne in the line. She was close to the front. Paul righted himself and climbed down to the ground.

"Hey, where're you going?" called Stephen.

"I'll be right back."

"If you bite anyone, don't get caught," called Stephen.

Paul laughed. He walked over to the swings and stood beside Suzanne.

"No cutting," called the boy behind Suzanne.

"I'm not in line," said Paul. "I'm just standing here."

A girl got off a swing, and Suzanne ran to it. Paul followed her.

Suzanne backed into the swing and took off with a *whoosh*. Forward and back, forward and back.

Paul rocked onto his toes, then back onto his heels each time Suzanne went by.

Forward and back, forward and back.

Suzanne twisted her neck to look at him. "If you're waiting for this swing, you have a long wait. I always swing the longest."

"I'm not waiting."

Forward and back, forward and back.

"You'd better get out of the way or I might hit you."

Paul stepped back a little.

Forward and back, forward and back.

She might never stop. And even if she did, she might not feel like talking to Paul. Maybe Paul didn't feel like talking, either. He turned around to go back to the monkey bars. "Ouch!" He looked everywhere. There was no one close.

"Did I hit you?" asked Suzanne. She dragged her feet till her swing stopped. "I told you to get out of the way."

"It wasn't you. I got pinched."

"Maybe a bee stung you. But just in case, you'd better stand a little to the side." Suzanne backed up and took off swinging again.

Paul rubbed his skin where he'd been pinched. He wondered if he had some crazy disease that just felt like a pinch. Maybe he was dying. Maybe he'd die and never have danced at all. He swallowed. "Do you really take ballet?"

"Yup," called Suzanne, flying by.

"Do you like it?"

"Yup."

"When's the class?"

"Saturday morning at ten. It's called 'Ballet One.'"

"Why are you talking about ballet?" said a voice behind Paul.

Paul turned around.

Stephen stomped his sneakers in the dry dirt.

"I just wanted to know."

"Boys don't do ballet," said Stephen.

"How do you know?"

"I have three sisters. I know everything about ballet." Stephen shook his head. "Boys don't do it."

"Why not?"

"Because it's for girls. Like my sisters." Stephen scooped up some dirt and dusted his palms. "Want to do the parallel bars?"

Angel Talk

Well done," said the Archangel of Courage. "That was a perfectly timed pinch."

"I know," said the little angel sadly. Paul needed it—what else could she do? "One more feather."

"What's the matter? You don't seem happy. But you're doing a terrific job. You can't expect Paul to grow bold overnight."

"I don't," said the little angel. She looked away.

The archangel put her hand under the little angel's chin and gently turned her head back to face her. "Do you maybe need the smallest pinch to help you speak up?"

The little angel looked into the archangel's encouraging eyes. "I don't want to let you down, but I really don't want to earn my wings so fast."

"But, why not? You can be an archangel, like me."

"I'm not like you," said the little angel. "You see children with problems and you know right away which little angels can help them and how. You just know. I can't do that. What if I misunderstood a child and picked the wrong little angel to help?"

"So you're frightened of becoming an archangel?"

"Yes."

"Well," said the archangel, "I didn't know that. See? I don't know everything. I look the situation over and I put together a child and a little angel almost by blind instinct and I simply hope for the best."

"Really?"

"Yes." The archangel smiled. "And sometimes I'm more than pleasantly surprised. The idea of pinching never occurred to me. But two

times in a row now, it's been just right for helping Paul."

The little angel gave a small smile. She had
to admit that deep down she was happy her
method was working.

"You've got good instincts, little angel."

Now if only I have the courage to keep act-
ing on them, thought the little angel.

Pinch Three

Sunlight made its way across Paul's pillow. It felt great on his cheeks. His eyes opened with a start. He looked at the clock: 9:35!

He peeked in Silvia's room. She was still asleep. One foot stuck out from under her covers. Paul remembered Stephen hanging on the jungle gym, talking about vampire bats. He gave Silvia's big toe a tiny bite.

Silvia sat up with a start.

"I'm going to watch Ballet One. Want to come?"

"Are you nuts? It's Saturday morning. Leave me alone." She flopped back down on the pillow.

Paul got dressed and brushed his teeth. Then he went into the kitchen and made himself toast with peanut butter. He could see Mom out in the backyard, cutting back the raspberry brambles. When he finished breakfast, he opened the door. "Hey, Mom, I'm going out."

Mom pushed her hair back and smiled at him. "Where're you going?"

"To see something. I'll be back soon."

"Well, all right. Just remember not to go past Elm Street."

Paul let the screen door swing shut and ran into the living room. He sat on the rocking chair and rocked fast as he put on his sneakers. That was always a challenge. But he had to stop rocking to tie them. Then he ran out the front door.

It was only four blocks to Camilla's School of Dance, so Paul made it there with five minutes to spare. As soon as he reached the top of the stairs, he took off his sneakers and hurried to his spot. But the bench was already full. Three mothers sat in a row, and a boy Paul's age sat on one end. A baby sat in a stroller by the other end of the bench.

Paul went over and stood by the end of the bench near the boy. He held his sneakers in his hands.

The boy wore a blue baseball cap and he didn't look at Paul. Even from here Paul could smell him—he smelled like strawberries. Paul glanced at him quickly. The boy chewed big and blew a huge pink bubble.

Girls in leotards came out of the dressing room. Paul looked carefully. Finally, Suzanne came out. She walked right onto the practice floor and began bending her legs in that way Silvia called a "plié."

Paul wanted to do pliés, but there were too many people around. He walked closer to the window.

"Ouch!" came a woman's voice.

Paul looked around.

It was Camilla, the dance teacher. She massaged her upper arm.

"Are you okay?" he asked.

"I don't know. I feel like someone just

pinched me." She smiled suddenly at Paul. "Well, it's you again. How nice. You going to take the class?"

Paul stepped backward. "I don't think so."

"Why not? You already have your shoes off. You can work with just your socks on today."

Paul hesitated. Then he put his shoes down and followed Camilla out onto the floor.

Angel Talk

That was a cheat." The Archangel of Courage crossed her arms at the chest.

The Little Angel of Courage looked up at her. "How so?"

"You pinched the ballet teacher, but she didn't need courage."

"How do you know?"

The Archangel of Courage lifted one eyebrow. "Since when do ballet teachers lack courage?"

"Maybe she didn't need courage exactly," said the Little Angel of Courage. "But if I hadn't pinched the ballet teacher, she might not have talked to Paul. And if she hadn't talked to Paul, he wouldn't have gotten up the courage to join the class today. So I had to do something. I had to. And pinching was the only thing I could think of." The little angel smiled. "My pinch did give Paul courage. Just indirectly."

The Archangel of Courage wrinkled her nose. "Okay, technically your pinch led to his courage. But the indirect delivery just doesn't feel right to me. The person who gets pinched should benefit somehow."

The Little Angel of Courage touched her two new feathers gingerly. They were truly beautiful. "When I pinched the ballet teacher, she noticed Paul and knew that she had to say something if she was going to help him. So really my pinch allowed her to help him. It made her a better person."

"I see what you mean. Sort of like two birds with one stone."

"Only my tool is a pinch."

The Archangel laughed. "You're earning wings to be an archangel of courage, not compassion. So your pinch to the teacher, while I admit it was a good thing for both of them, counts only once—for the courage it gave Paul." The Archangel of Courage tapped the little angel's wing. A third feather grew.

"Oh!" The little angel looked at the new feather in dismay. "I wasn't arguing that I deserved a feather. I just thought you were angry at me for interfering with the teacher when Paul is my assignment."

"I know that. But you did earn this feather." The Archangel of Courage did a demi-plié. "You're a clever one, little angel."

The Giraffe

The class worked on feet. First position, with toes pointing out. Second position, with feet spread apart.

And on arms.

And on bending from the waist.

Paul worked and worked.

The girl beside Paul slid her feet apart and leaned down far. She looked so much like a giraffe drinking water that Paul could hardly believe his eyes.

The girl stretched her neck farther. She swayed ever so slightly.

"You're a giraffe," said Paul.

"What?" The girl stood up again quickly, and now she wasn't a giraffe anymore. "Are you talking to me?"

Paul smiled sheepishly and concentrated

on his own bending. This was the second time he'd seen a dancer as an animal. Maybe he was going crazy.

At the end of class, Camilla handed Paul a folded piece of paper. "Give this to your parents."

Paul walked home, clutching the paper. Camilla hadn't said he couldn't read it. So he might as well. He unfolded it.

Dear Kane family,
Paul joined our Ballet One class today. He did excellent work. If you would like him to enroll, please dress him in black tights, black ballet shoes, and a white T-shirt. I hope to see him next week.
Camilla

When Paul came in the front door, he spied Dad at the kitchen table. He put Camilla's note in his pocket. "Hi, Dad."

Dad put down the newspaper he was reading. "Where've you been?"

"Look." Paul walked forward slowly, moving his arms through first position, then second, then third. Then he let his arms trail behind him. "What am I?"

"What do you mean?"

Paul slid his feet apart and leaned down as far as he could. He swayed to one side, then the other. "What am I now?"

Dad cocked his head. "Am I supposed to guess?"

Paul straightened up in a hurry. "What do you know about *Swan Lake*, Dad?"

"Is that around here?"

"It's the name of a ballet."

"Oh. Yeah, I remember now. I think the swan dies or something."

"That's right. Do you know if there are any famous ballets with giraffes in them?"

"I don't really know much about ballet. I've heard of ballets with fawns and cats and even spiders and butterflies, so there might be a ballet with a giraffe."

Paul sat down beside his father. "Do you like ballet, Dad?"

"Sure. Why do you ask?"

"No reason." Paul looked at Dad's plate. "Are you going to finish your bagel?"

"You can have it. What's all this talk about ballet?"

"Nothing." Paul chewed the bagel. When he finished, he just sat there.

"What's wrong?"

"Nothing's wrong."

"You never sit beside me silently." Dad rubbed his chin. "Is something on your mind?"

"Maybe." Paul took Camilla's note out of his pocket. He handed it to Dad.

Dad opened it and read. "I didn't know you could dance."

"I just started."

"How'd it go?"

"Okay, I think."

Dad reread the note. Then he gave a little jump. He looked around in confusion, and his eyes settled on Paul. He took out his car keys. "Looks like we've got some shopping to do."

Angel Talk

The little angel was so excited, her hands flew crazy in front of the archangel's face. "You pinched him, didn't you? You pinched that dad."

The Archangel of Courage caught the little angel's hands and smiled. "Good guess."

The little angel jumped in place. "I knew it. But why did you pinch him? Was it like me pinching the dance teacher? Did you do it to help Paul indirectly?"

"No. Paul's your job. I did it to help the dad. He had second thoughts—he needed a little courage of his own."

"But, why? What's scary about buying Paul ballet clothes?"

"Nothing, I hope. But you never know."

The Duck

Paul and Stephen finished their milk and crushed the cartons. Then they stood a good six feet back from the big, wire wastebasket and tossed them. Both of them made it in.

"Yes!" said Stephen.

The lunchroom teacher frowned and walked toward them.

Stephen waved at her. "Hurry, Paul."

They ran out the side door of the lunchroom and onto the playground. Lunch recess was Paul's favorite because it was the longest recess of the day.

Stephen grabbed a basketball from the supply shed. He tossed it to Paul. Paul tossed it back.

"You're good at ballet, Paul."

Paul jerked his head to the side.

Suzanne stood there.

"Boys don't do ballet," said Stephen. He tossed the ball.

Paul caught it. He threw the ball up as high as he could. It came down with a *splat* in the puddle beside him.

"Paul does," said Suzanne.

Stephen came up to Paul. "What's she talking about?"

Paul rubbed the muddy ball on his jacket. "I take lessons."

"What? Ballet lessons?"

"Yes."

"Since when?"

"Saturday," said Suzanne. "He was at my class."

"You can't." Stephen's voice rose in a shout.

Paul was confused. Why was Stephen angry? He tossed the ball to Stephen.

"You're a sissy," shouted Stephen.

Paul blinked back tears. "You don't know what you're talking about."

"Boys don't do ballet. Even my sisters say they don't. Anyway, you're too clumsy. You walk like a duck."

Paul kept blinking. "Oh, yeah? Well, you'll never be a swan."

"A swan?"

"And you'll never be a giraffe, either." Paul's throat was tight, and his cheeks burned.

"You're crazy!" Stephen shook his head and ran off with the ball.

Suzanne put her hands in her pockets. "Sorry."

Paul shrugged. "It's okay."

"Your mom's going to be angry at how dirty you got your jacket."

Paul blinked again.

"Come on," said Suzanne. "I'll help you clean it in the water fountain."

Angel Talk

The Little Angel of Courage shook her head. "I'm sorry."

The archangel came close. "About what?"

"I should have done something. But I didn't know what. I was afraid I'd do the wrong thing—so I did nothing." The little angel covered her face with her hands. "I left Paul all on his own."

The archangel put her arm around the little angel. "Sometimes doing nothing is the right thing to do."

The little angel dropped her hands. "But Paul made a mess of things. Stephen had no idea what he meant with that talk about swans and giraffes."

"So what? Paul knew what he was saying. He stuck up for himself—and he knows that.

That's what matters." The archangel tightened her hold. "He's learning about courage, little angel. You're teaching him."

The little angel hugged the archangel and hoped very hard that she was right.

The Non-Duck

The rest of the week Paul stayed in from recess. On Tuesday he helped Ms. Berkowitz arrange the items on the nature table. On Wednesday he cleaned all the blackboards and beat out the erasers. On Thursday he built an airplane out of plastic connecting blocks. On Friday he designed a racing car out of those blocks—a car with huge wheels and a driver's seat that swiveled in a full circle. That way, if the car turned over, it could keep on going and the driver could keep on driving because the seat would just flip over, too. It was neat.

Paul kept himself so busy, he hardly had any time at all to miss Stephen.

And each night he went into his parents' bedroom and walked around, looking at

himself in their tall mirror. He didn't waddle like a duck. Did he?

Saturday it rained.

Paul stood at the living room window. Dad stood beside him. "I was thinking, Dad. Maybe I won't go to ballet today."

"I'll give you a ride, sport. How's that sound?"

Paul looked down at his feet. "Stephen says boys don't do ballet."

"Where'd he get that idea from?"

"His sisters told him. He called me a sissy."

"I was afraid this would happen," said Dad. "Well, Stephen's just plain wrong. Some of the most famous ballet dancers are men."

"Like who?"

"Balanchine and Nureyev and Baryshnikov."

"I thought you didn't know much about ballet."

"I don't. But everyone knows about them. Like I said, they're famous."

"They sound foreign."

"They are. And Balanchine's dead, I think."

"Oh."

Dad furrowed his brow. "You know, Paul, there have to be lots of men ballet dancers. Otherwise, who would the ballerinas dance with?"

"Yeah, I guess you're right."

"And a lot of them are American. And a lot of them are alive."

Paul walked in front of Dad. "Am I a duck, Dad?"

"Quack," said Dad.

"What's that mean?"

"That you're not a duck. If you were, you'd know what it meant."

Paul grinned.

"Go get dressed, non-duck. It's duck weather out. Non-ducks like you need a ride. Where'd I put my car keys?"

Angel Talk

ou let that father do a lot of your work for you," said the Archangel of Courage.

The Little Angel of Courage smiled. "I knew I could count on him. Especially since you made him brave. And I'm trying to see if I can get Paul all the way there with only one more pinch."

"Why?"

"I only need two more feathers to earn my wings. So if I help Paul with just one more feather, I'll have one feather left to earn. That gives me a little more time before I become an archangel."

"So you're still worrying about that? Wouldn't you like to make Paul fly in his own way at the same time you fly? Don't you think that would be lovely?"

"It might be lovely," said the little angel, "but I'd rather wait."

The Archangel of Courage pursed her lips. "Be careful, little angel. Courage is a delicate matter. If you don't give it when it's needed, everything you've worked so hard for could be lost."

Pinch Four

Paul ran up the stairs of the ballet school. When he reached the top, he went right to the bench and took off his sneakers.

The boy in the blue baseball cap from the week before was sitting on the bench again. But the mothers hadn't sat down yet.

"Are you going to take class again today?" asked the boy.

Paul didn't look at the boy. He didn't care what this stranger thought of him. After all, if Paul could take Stephen making fun of him, he could take anything. And, anyway, the boy smelled again. Grape this time. Who cared what a smelly kid thought of him?

"Are you?" asked the boy, popping his purple gum. "Are you going to take class?"

"Yes." Paul shoved his sneakers under the bench.

A woman came over and sat down at the far end of the bench.

Paul glanced at her as he took his brand-new ballet shoes out of his tote.

The boy was still looking at him, and blowing a huge bubble.

Paul didn't like the idea of this boy watching him get ready. "Why don't you go sit by your mother?"

"Who? Her? She's not my mother. I come with my little sister. Missy. Her real name's Melissa. She's in the class before this one. I walk her here because the class starts too early for my mother. We have a baby at home now. John-John. His real name's Jonathan. But he isn't thin at all. He's plump. So his name is all wrong for him. He should be Jonaplump. He makes Mom late for everything. But after class Mom comes with John-John and she walks Missy home. So I get to stick around."

Paul stared at the boy. He'd never heard anyone talk so fast in his life—especially while chewing gum. But it looked like the boy was finished now. "Why do you want to?"

"Why do I want to what?"

"Why do you want to stick around?" Paul asked.

"I don't know."

Paul was surprised. He'd expected another long string of words.

Paul thought about that. The boy watched ballet class. And he didn't want to talk about why. Paul used to watch ballet class.

Paul was about to sit on the floor to put on his shoes when he felt a little pinch on his pinky toe. "Want to take class today?" he asked suddenly.

"No," said the boy. "There're only a few weeks till the class ends, anyway. My mom says there isn't enough time for me to learn all the stuff you need to know for the recital at the end."

"It's not hard. I just started, too, and I already know most of it." Paul put on his right ballet shoe and looked up at the boy. "I could help you."

The boy chomped on his gum for a moment. "I don't have the right shoes today, anyway."

"Go in your socks. I did that last week."

The boy didn't answer.

Paul stood up and handed the boy a ballet shoe. "Here, you wear my left shoe and I'll wear my right shoe."

The boy smiled and put on the shoe. "I'm Richie. Richard, really."

Angel Talk

Well, now. You pinched Paul, all right, but this time, the one who got the courage to do what he really wanted was Richie."

The Little Angel of Courage nodded. "I know. It was funny watching them try to dance with one ballet shoe each."

"Neither of them did very well," said the archangel. "Paul didn't think that one through."

The little angel smiled at the memory. "Maybe he did. Paul knew just how scared Richie was. So he had to do something super kind, even if it meant that then he wouldn't be able to dance as well. I think it made him feel good to know he was helping Paul."

The Archangel of Courage looked at the little angel for a long time. "You're right. You're so,

so right. Paul felt bold today. Giving courage to Richie helped him feel brave." The archangel examined the little angel's wings. "Let's see, now, where should this feather go?"

"Wait," said the little angel. "Since it was Richie who got the courage, I shouldn't get a feather this time."

"You deserve one." The Archangel of Courage held her finger poised over a bare spot on the little angel's left wing. "What do you say?"

How could she turn down a feather? Feathers were so beautiful. And the Little Angel of Courage was clever, that's what the archangel had said. She would find a way to get Paul there without any more pinches. "Okay."

The archangel touched her wing, and a new feather grew.

Animals

In the next three weeks, the class worked hard. There was a lot to learn, after all.

They did kicks. First low, then a little higher, then as high as they could do it. They kicked to the front and to the side and to the back. They kicked with feet parallel and they kicked with toes pointed out. Paul was good at it.

They did turns. Paul learned to keep his eyes focused where he was going. When he turned, he kept looking at a spot straight ahead, then whipped his head around at the last moment and fixed his eyes on that spot again. That was called "spotting," and it was supposed to keep him from getting dizzy. It sort of worked. They did turns across the floor diagonally. They did turns in lines. They did turns all around the edge of the dance floor.

They did rolls. Forward and backward. Shoulder rolls and sideways rolls. Rolls with their bodies curled and rolls with their bodies like logs. They even rolled on top of one another.

And they did leaps. Paul loved the leaps best of all. He did them extra long.

There would be a part in their recital when each person got to do a favorite move. So for the last five minutes of the class, Camilla let them practice whatever they wanted.

Richie zipped past Paul, twirling and twirling, and as he twirled he seemed to turn into a bumblebee. Buzz-buzz-buzz. Paul gaped.

Suzanne rolled in a circle around Paul and, as she rolled, she turned into a monkey. Paul stared.

After class, Paul always went home and stood before the tall mirror. He did all the things they did in class. But in front of the mirror, he was always Paul—he never turned into an animal.

Silvia became a swan when she danced. Richie became a bumblebee. Suzanne became a monkey.

But Paul stayed Paul.

At least he wasn't a duck, like Stephen had said.

Still, he wanted to be something more, something wonderful on the dance floor.

Angel Talk

Why does Paul stand around watching everyone else during the last five minutes of ballet class?" asked the little angel.

"They all become animals in his eyes. Didn't you know that?"

"Sure I knew that. But what I don't understand is why he doesn't join them."

"Maybe he's not confident that he has a dancing animal inside him. He might need a pinch of courage."

The little angel looked away. How long could Paul go before she'd have to pinch him?

The Mouse

Finally the morning of the recital came. Paul had decided last week what he was going to do in the part of the dance where each person did their favorite move. So everything would go fine.

He put on his new yellow tights. And on top he wore a yellow shirt instead of his usual white. Richie was going to wear yellow, too. Camilla had decided the two boys should match. The girls in the class were going to wear their usual pink leotards, but to make them look special they added little, filmy pink skirts. Paul thought they looked great in the dress rehearsal.

Paul ran downstairs and into the kitchen. He poured a big bowl of cereal and cut a banana into it. He wanted a big breakfast so he'd have energy.

Silvia came into the kitchen. She was

dressed in brown. "Here. Would you pin this tail on me?"

Paul pinned the tail on her. "Are you a donkey?"

"A donkey! No. What a terrible thing to say."

"I didn't mean anything. It just looks like a donkey tail."

"Well, it's not. It's a *mouse* tail. We're doing a dance from *The Nutcracker.*"

"Oh. I've heard of *The Nutcracker.*"

"Of course you have." Silvia took a bowl from the cupboard and sat down beside Paul. "It's famous."

"But I didn't know it was about mice."

"Well, it's not just about mice. It's about a lot of things. But this is one of the best dances because there's a sword fight between the Mouse King and the Nutcracker. The mice all have to run around terrified. What dance are you doing?"

"I don't know. I don't think it has a name. We just dance." Paul took a big mouthful of cereal.

Silvia looked at her empty bowl. Then she looked at Paul. "How can you eat?"

"Huh? I'm hungry."

"Aren't you nervous?" Silvia pushed her bowl away. "It's so exciting. Everyone will be watching."

Paul gobbled Cheerios faster and faster. He imagined the audience full of smiling mothers and fathers. "Mom and Dad will love it."

"I know. But they love everything. It's the other people that make me nervous. Anna and Margaret will be watching."

"How come?"

"I invited them. Didn't you invite anyone?"

"Nope."

"Well, that's okay. Stephen will be there, anyway."

"Stephen?" Paul dropped his spoon. "Who invited Stephen?"

"His sisters are in it. He's bound to come."

Paul stood up. "I guess I'm not that hungry after all."

Angel Talk

The little angel's hands flew around again, but this time out of worry, not excitement. "Did you know Stephen was coming?"

"I assumed he was," said the archangel. "We both knew his sisters take ballet."

"Well, I didn't assume it. Poor Paul."

"I have confidence in you. You can help him through it."

But can I do it without a pinch? wondered the little angel. Poor Paul. And poor me.

Pinch Five and So Many More

Paul stood in the wing of the stage, squashed between Richie and Suzanne. Richie smelled like honey. Was that some new kind of gum?

Suzanne pointed at the kids dancing on the stage. It was the Beginner Ballet class. She whispered, "Aren't they cute?"

Paul couldn't begin to think about the beginner class. He realized suddenly that he didn't remember anything he was supposed to do on the stage. Nothing at all. His stomach became an ice block. He should run away now.

But the familiar piano tune blasted out. Richie and Suzanne ran to their places. Paul was pulled along by the motion all around him.

He stared out past the stage edge. He couldn't see anything, just an ocean of blurry

faces. Then he saw a hand waving. It was Mom. And beside her sat Dad. Paul wanted to run to them and beg them to take him home. Right now.

Paul jumped. Someone had pinched him on the bottom. He was sure of it. But it helped him forget his stage fright, so he pinched himself on both arms, on his sides, on his legs. He looked again at Mom and Dad. They were smiling, looking forward to seeing Paul dance.

Paul gave himself one last pinch. He was ready. He would dance his best and think only of Mom and Dad. Who cared if Stephen was there? Mom and Dad were watching.

The dancers formed three lines on the stage. They leaned and kicked and turned. Then the lines became three circles. Everybody took turns twirling to the center of the circle and then back again.

And now was the time when they each broke from the rest, one at a time, and did their own favorite move around the outside of their circle. The flute played loud, and Richie zipped by, the best bumblebee ever. The drums banged, and Suzanne rolled by, the best monkey ever.

And now it was Paul's turn. The bells rang out, and he leaped around the circle, higher than ever before. His legs stretched farther than ever. His body felt stronger than ever.

Before Paul could even catch his breath, the dance was over. Suzanne squeezed Paul's hand and smiled wide. Richie squeezed Paul's other hand and smiled wide. The whole class bowed together on the count of three. The audience clapped and clapped. Paul wanted to leap for joy.

Angel Talk

He did it!" said the newest Archangel of Courage.

The Archangel of Courage smiled. "Because you did it."

The newest Archangel of Courage stretched her wings. "I'm ashamed it took me so long to give him that final pinch."

"You were afraid of earning your wings. I know that." The Archangel of Courage smoothed her own wings. "And that's why you'll make a wonderful archangel of courage."

"What do you mean?"

"Being brave enough to do something you're afraid of to help someone else is the best kind of courage."

One Last Animal

After the recital Paul ran up the aisle to Mom and Dad.

Mom hugged Paul. "You were great."

Dad hugged Paul. "The best."

"What about me?" Silvia yanked at Dad's shirt. "I had a hard part."

Daddy swung Silvia around. "You were terrific."

"Fantastic," said Mom. "When we get home, you have to show me that special kick you do."

"Hey, Paul!"

Paul recognized Stephen's voice, of course. His breath quickened. He looked down and pretended not to hear.

Stephen grabbed Paul by the arm. "I saw you jump."

"Leap," said Paul, keeping his eyes on the

ground.

"Wow, you went high."

Paul looked up in amazement. Stephen was smiling. "You'll be a champion basketball player. I can't believe how far you leaped, too. Like a lion."

A lion? Right!

Stephen jumped. "How's this look?"

Paul smiled. "Well, I move a little as I do it. I sort of run and jump at the same time."

Stephen jump-leaped. He crashed into a seat and burst out laughing.

Paul laughed, too. "With the right ballet shoes, you could be a lion leaper, too."

"Ballet shoes are for dancers," said Stephen. "Like you. I'll just be a ballplayer." He bounced an imaginary ball on the ground, then did a jump shot at an imaginary hoop. "Want to go to the court? We can play ball or something." He tossed Paul the imaginary ball.

Paul leaped, caught it, and threw it back. "Sure."

Angel Thoughts

The newest Archangel of Courage flew round and round the basketball court. It seemed funny to her now that she'd never noticed the bells in that dance that Paul practiced so many times. She'd never noticed them until they rang for her.

Ah, there were the boys now. They were bouncing a basketball back and forth between them.

This task was truly done.

Now it was time to find the next. She flew off in search of a child in need of courage and the right little angel for the task. Her instincts would help her make the match.

Beginning Ballet

Professional dancers have to practice every day. One exercise that they usually start with is called a *plié* (pronounced plee-ay). Dancers do pliés using all five ballet foot positions. These two drawings show Paul in the fifth foot position.

Meet the Little Angel of Generosity
in the next **Aladdin Angelwings**

№. 5 Give and Take

Angel Talk

The Little Angel of Generosity smoothed the sheet of wrapping paper flat. Then he carefully rolled the yo-yo up into the paper. He didn't have ribbon, but the white twine did just fine. He tied a firm knot and stayed squatting, with his arms crossed at his chest, viewing his handiwork. A pile of five presents for his four best friends, plus one extra—for himself. After all, he loved yo-yos, too.

"Are they for a party?" asked the Archangel of Generosity.

"Oh, I didn't see you there." The little angel jumped to his feet. "No, they're just for fun."

The archangel smiled and picked up the spool of twine. She played with the loose end. "Only five. Are these for little angels?"

"Yes. Including me." The little angel gave a small yank on the archangel's sleeve. "Why are you here? Have you got a task for me?"

The Archangel of Generosity lined up the presents in a neat row. "Nothing for the archangels?"

"Archangels don't need anything."

The archangel put her hands on her hips. "Who says?"

The little angel laughed. "Come on. You can have anything you want, anytime you want it."

"Can I have one of these presents?"

"No," yelped the little angel. "I only have five."

"Well, then, I can't have anything I want after all, can I?"

The Little Angel of Generosity screwed up his mouth. "What's your point?"

"Think about it."

"You wouldn't even like what's in the wrapping paper," said the little angel. "It's for kids. Plus, it's not a girl thing anyway."

"How do you know?" asked the archangel. "Think about that, too. But in the meantime, you're right: I do have a task for you."

"Great." The little angel grinned wide. "All I need is one more task, and a bell will ring because I'll have enough feathers to earn my wings."

The Archangel of Generosity rubbed the back of her neck in thought. "Why do you accept the tasks I ask you to do? Is it just for the pleasure of earning wings?"

The little angel gasped. "How can you ask that?"

"I just want you to think about why you do things."

"Well, I know the answer to this one for sure," said the little angel. "I do the tasks because I want to help children."

"So you don't care about your wings?"

"Yes, I care. I want my wings a lot. I can't wait to hear the bell that will ring when I earn them. I'll fly everywhere. But that's just a nice extra. A wonderful extra. The real point is to help children."

"Good," said the archangel. "Let's go help someone."

Art

"I already know what I'm getting." Setha clasped her hands behind her back and rocked from foot to foot.

"You look like a penguin," said Dinah quietly.

Setha kept rocking, her hands still behind her back. "It's so terrific. Mommy bought all these art materials. I'm getting a five-pound box of clay. I can make pinch pots and coil bowls and anything I want."

Dinah kicked the toe of her sneaker into the dirt. "If you dig in the right spots, you can find clay. You don't have to buy it."

"Not like this clay. It's self-hardening. I don't even need a kiln."

Dinah dug deeper with her sneaker. "The ground is hard here. I think there's clay right beneath our feet."

"Gray clay, yuck. The clay Mommy bought me is red-brown. It's from Mexico and it's so beautiful, Dinah, you wouldn't believe it." Setha swayed her head from side to side as though she were listening to private music inside her head. Her braid swung in a wide arc. "And Mommy even got me the acrylic paints I wanted. They go perfect on clay. I can decorate whatever I make."

"Why buy colored clay if you're only going to paint it other colors?"

"I won't paint every inch. Just patterns. And acrylics are the best. They're so bright, they look like plastic. The set has eight colors. Eight."

Dinah looked from her best friend to the ground. Red-brown clay that hardened all by itself was something wonderful. "How much did it cost?"

"The set of acrylics?"

"No, the clay."

"I don't know. Mommy bought me water-color paints, too. And the right kind of paper for them. And these great brushes that hold a fine point when you get the tip wet. I don't know how much any of it costs and I don't care. It's for my birthday."

Dinah smiled. "You're a good artist."

"I'm not so good yet. But I'm going to be." Setha caught her long braid, pulled it forward over her shoulder, and played with the tips of it. "You need new sneakers."

Dinah looked down. The sole of her right shoe was separating from the top at the toe end. "Maybe I'll ask my dad for sneakers for my birthday. But that's not for a few months yet."

"I know. So . . . ?" Setha's voice rose in a question.

"So what?"

Setha laughed. "So what are you getting me for mine? Mine is next week."

Dinah blinked. "I can't tell you. You need at least one surprise."

"I'll get plenty of surprises. Daddy always surprises me. And so does Lil."

Lil was Setha's big sister. She was usually pretty nice to Setha. Dinah liked her. Lil was bound to get Setha something really nice.

Dinah had no idea what she'd get Setha— or where she'd find the money to get Setha anything she'd really like. "Well, I'll surprise you, too."

Don't miss these other
Aladdin *Angelwings* stories:

№ 5
Give and Take

№ 6
No Fair!

№ 7
April Flowers